Happy
Butterfly

by Pippa Goodhart

Illustrated by Lauren Tobia

W
FRANKLIN WATTS
LONDON•SYDNEY

First published in 2009 by
Franklin Watts
338 Euston Road
London
NW1 3BH

Franklin Watts Australia
Level 17/207 Kent Street
Sydney
NSW 2000

A CIP catalogue record for this book is available
from the British Library.

ISBN 978 0 7496 8513 3 (hbk)
ISBN 978 0 7496 8519 5 (pbk)

Series Editor: Jackie Hamley
Editor: Melanie Palmer
Series Advisor: Dr Hilary Minns
Series Designer: Peter Scoulding

Printed in China

Franklin Watts is a division of
Hachette Children's Books,
an Hachette UK company.
www.hachette.co.uk

Happy heard a band.
"I want to see it!"
she said.

3

Just then a butterfly
flew down in front
of Happy.

Then it flew up again.

"Lucky butterfly!"
said Happy.

"Would you like to be
a butterfly?"asked
Grandma Gloria.

Grandma took
Happy shopping.

8

They got wire
and netting.

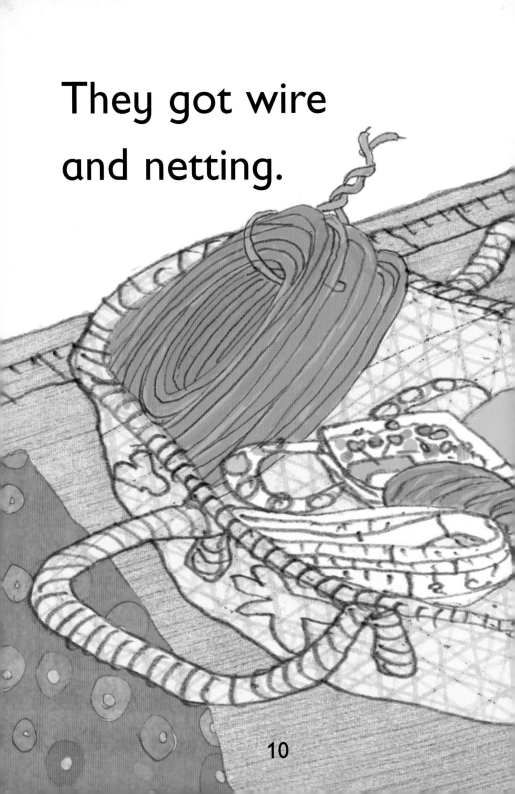

They got sparkles.

They got beads.

Grandma Gloria
made wings.

Happy stuck on sparkles
and beads.

They made a head
band together.

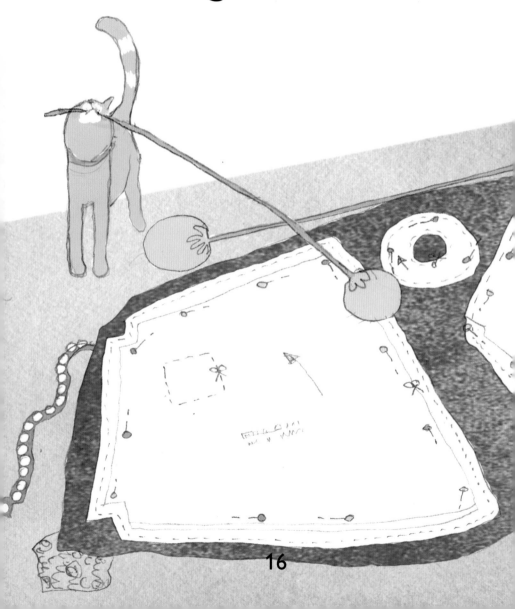

"Look at me, I'm a butterfly!" said Happy.

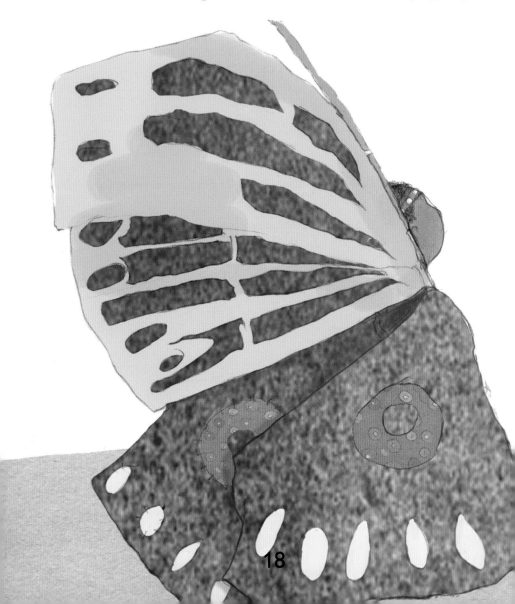

This time, Happy saw everything!

20

21

Puzzle Time!

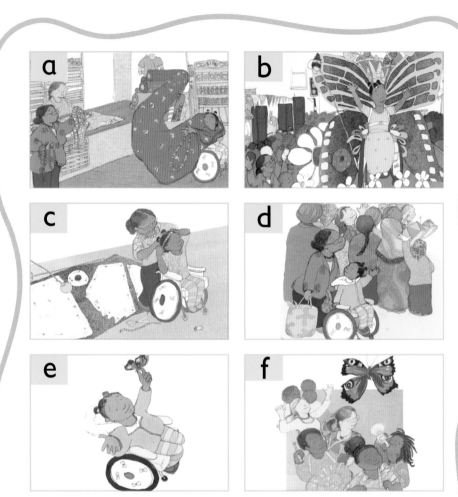

Put these pictures in the right order and retell the story!

cheerful

sad

upset

proud

Which words describe Happy
at the beginning of the story?
Which words describe
her at the end?

Turn over for answers!

Notes for adults

TADPOLES are structured to provide support for newly independent readers. The stories may also be used by adults for sharing with young children.

Starting to read alone can be daunting. **TADPOLES** help by providing visual support and repeating words and phrases. These books will both develop confidence and encourage reading and rereading for pleasure.

If you are reading this book with a child, here are a few suggestions:

1. Make reading fun! Choose a time to read when you and the child are relaxed and have time to share the story.
2. Talk about the story before you start reading. Look at the cover and the blurb. What might the story be about? Why might the child like it?
3. Encourage the child to retell the story, using the jumbled picture puzzle as a starting point. Extend vocabulary with the matching words to characters puzzle.
4. Discuss the story and see if the child can relate it to their own experience.
5. Give praise! Remember that small mistakes need not always be corrected.

Answers

Here is the correct order!

1.d 2.e 3.f 4.a 5.c 6.b

Words to describe Happy
at the beginning:
sad, upset

Words to describe Happy
at the end:
cheerful, proud